DRAGON STORM 5

KAI AND BONESHADOW

Alastair Chisholm

illustrated by Eric Deschamps

A STEPPING STONE BOOK™

Random House 🏠 New York

CONTENTS

Text copyright © 2022 by Alastair Chisholm
Cover art copyright © 2022 by Ben Mantle
Interior illustrations copyright © 2022 by Eric Deschamps

All rights reserved. Published in the United States by Random House Children's Books, a division of Penguin Random House LLC, New York. Originally published in paperback in slightly different form in the United Kingdom by Nosy Crow, Ltd, London, in 2022.

Random House and the colophon are registered trademarks and A Stepping Stone Book and the colophon are trademarks of Penguin Random House LLC.

Visit us on the Web!
rhcbooks.com

Educators and librarians, for a variety of teaching tools, visit us at RHTeachersLibrarians.com

Library of Congress Cataloging-in-Publication Data is available upon request.
ISBN 978-0-593-65010-3 (trade) — ISBN 978-0-593-65011-0 (lib. bdg.) — ISBN 978-0-593-65012-7 (ebook)

Printed in the United States of America
10 9 8 7 6 5 4 3 2 1
First American Edition

IN THE LAND OF DRACONIS, THERE ARE NO DRAGONS.

Once, there were. Once, humans
and dragons were friends and guarded
the land. They were wise, and strong, and
created the great city of Rivven together.

But then came the Dragon Storm, and the
dragons retreated from the world
of humans. To the citizens of Draconis,
they became legend and myth.

And so, these days, in the land of Draconis,
there are no dragons. . . .

Or so people thought.

1
KAI

Under the heart of Rivven was a cave. Hardly anyone in the city knew it existed, and even fewer knew how to find it. Yet it was huge— a cavern so vast that you could hardly see from one end to the other. Softly glowing lamps hung from its roof like tiny suns. They shone down on a world that was a home, a training ground, a school, and a place of secrets.

DRAGON STORM

It was the Dragonseer Guild Hall, and today it was a racecourse.

"Come on, Boneshadow!" called Kai as they hurtled around the track. "You're doing great!"

He glanced back as they reached the second bend. Behind him was Erin, then Tom and Connor almost neck and neck, then the others. Kai was leading, but they were only halfway around.

"How are you feeling?" he called down.

Beneath him, Boneshadow let out a laugh. "Wonderful!" she cried.

Kai tucked his head and grinned. He was in a saddle and his feet were secure in stirrups, but it wasn't a horse he was riding. This creature's skin was smooth and dry and as white as bone. She had a long neck and a large head, and on her chest was a red flare. Kai sat tucked between two folded wings.

She was Boneshadow, and she was a *dragon*.

"Rockhammer's gaining on us!" Kai called. Behind him, Erin's dragon, Rockhammer, was huge and fierce-looking, with great spikes. The ground shuddered with her every stride. Erin's face had a look of grim determination.

"He'll get tired," Boneshadow told Kai. "Hold on!"

They raced around the curve. Kai could feel Boneshadow's powerful muscles move. He could sense the beat of her heart, the joy of running, the feeling that she could keep going forever. He could feel all this because, like the other children, he was a *dragonseer*. Boneshadow was his dragon, and he was her human.

The pathway straightened, and Boneshadow stretched her legs. The air whistled through Kai's short black hair and made his brown eyes water. He blinked and laughed. The ground shuddered, and he realized that Rockhammer was catching up with them. The big dragon was faster on the straightaway, where his long legs could make up the distance. Ahead of them was the next fence. Boneshadow adjusted her pace.

"Ready?" she growled. Kai held on tight, and the dragon bunched her hind legs. She *leaped* over the fence, landing with hardly a jolt. On her back, the leathery white wings stayed folded.

Like many dragons, Boneshadow could fly, but this was a running race only. Kai felt the *thump* behind him as Rockhammer leaped and cleared the fence too. He could hear Erin bellowing and knew they were right behind—but already the next bend was coming up. Boneshadow nimbly leaned into the curve and pulled away again.

Rockhammer caught them on the third straightaway, coming up to the last corner. Kai could tell he was tired, and his big pink tongue flopped around in his mouth like a dog's. The finish line was approaching, and Boneshadow was just ahead. If they could make the corner, Kai knew his dragon would have energy for the final sprint!

Erin shouted something into Rockhammer's ear, and the big dragon nodded. He started to drift sideways, into Boneshadow's line. Kai glanced at him in alarm.

"Hey!" he yelled.

The big dragon was very close, almost brushing against them. Five yards . . .

"Whoa!" Kai called. Boneshadow eased up immediately, and with a whoop Erin and Rockhammer edged them out and pulled ahead. Now they were in the lead, and Boneshadow had lost her pace. She accelerated as they came into the final stretch, almost catching up, but Rockhammer extended his long neck and crossed the finish line first.

"YASSSSSS!" shouted Erin. Rockhammer gave a huge bellow.

DRAGON STORM

Behind them, Kai and Boneshadow slowed to a stop. Kai slid down from his dragon's back and patted her.

"Sorry, Bone," he said with a rueful smile. "If we'd gone for the turn, we would have crashed into Rockhammer."

Boneshadow shook her large white head. "We were ahead of them," she said softly. "They should have let us go first."

"I know," said Kai. "But I didn't want to take the risk. Anyway, the race was fun even if we didn't win, right?"

Boneshadow chuckled and rested her head against Kai's shoulder. "Of course," she said. "But I'm not sure Vice Chancellor Creedy agrees."

Kai looked up. Striding toward them were two of the senior Guild members. Vice Chancellor Creedy was dressed all in gray and had a big frown on his face. Beside him was Daisy, who taught self-defense. She walked with a bouncing, happy stride, in bright-yellow leggings that seemed to glow in comparison with Creedy's dull robes.

"Boy!" snapped Creedy, pointing at Kai. "What was that?"

Kai blinked. "Um . . . Well, sir, I didn't want—"

"You let up," said Creedy. "You had the lead and you let up!" He scowled. "This isn't a *game*, you know. The purpose of these races is to learn how to deal with high-pressure

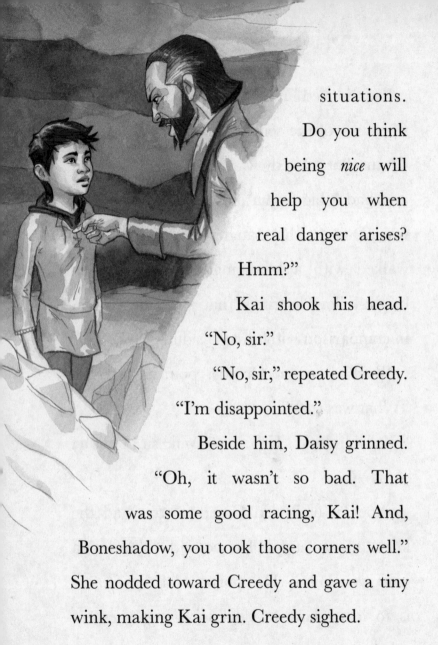

situations. Do you think being *nice* will help you when real danger arises? Hmm?"

Kai shook his head. "No, sir."

"No, sir," repeated Creedy. "I'm disappointed."

Beside him, Daisy grinned. "Oh, it wasn't so bad. That was some good racing, Kai! And, Boneshadow, you took those corners well." She nodded toward Creedy and gave a tiny wink, making Kai grin. Creedy sighed.

"That's it," he said irritably, waving a hand. "That's enough for today. Put away your harnesses—*neatly* now!"

Kai and Boneshadow headed back to the training ground. Ahead of them, Erin was doing a victory dance. Rockhammer was walking in a great swagger with his huge mouth open and grinning.

"It *was* a good race," said Boneshadow.

"Yeah," said Kai.

Would have been good to win, though, he thought.

2

DINNER

Kai carefully folded up Boneshadow's harness and packed it in one of the chests by the training ground. Erin had left hers on the floor, and Kai put it away before walking to the dining hut with Tom, his best friend.

"Good race!" said Tom. He'd come in third on his dragon, Ironskin. Tom was taller and bigger than Kai. He was a blacksmith's son, wide-shouldered and strong, while Kai was slim. Ironskin was tall and broad too, and her skin was a deep, dark red, with bright lines like fire in a forge. She and Tom were alike in personality—both were loyal and protective.

"Did Creedy give you a hard time?" asked Tom.

Kai shrugged. He didn't really let it bother him. Some people got worked up about things, but Kai was always able to let them wash over him. "No, he was fine."

Tom laughed and shook his head. "You're too nice, Kai," he said.

Kai smiled. "Funny, that's what Creedy said too."

They reached the hut, and Kai turned to Boneshadow. "See you later," he said.

Boneshadow nodded. She then faded away until she was completely gone. Beside her, Ironskin did the same.

The dragons were from a different world, a world that was hard to imagine. Drun, who taught summoning, called it a world of *ideas*. "Every dragon is different," he'd say. "They each got their own shape, their own way of bein'. You're dragonseers, and that means you all got the power to reach into their world and make a connection. And if they want, they can come across. And when they do, their shape, the way they are . . . comes from *you*."

Kai could still feel the faint whisper of that connection in his mind, and he smiled. He and Tom entered the hut and sat down for dinner.

Hilda, the cook, was serving a rich potato pie. It was the perfect meal after a day of exercise, and the children started eating right away.

There was Cara, pale and thin, sitting very still as she liked to do. Cara often kept to herself, but today she was looking at one of Ellis's maps. Ellis was showing Cara routes, drawing them carefully with a pencil. Beside Cara was Mira, who was short and bursting with energy. Her long black hair was tied back, and as usual, her face was smeared with oil. Mira loved tinkering with machinery. Across from Ellis, Connor was reading a book. Erin, tall and athletic, sat at the head of the table. She looked pleased with herself as she retold the story about how she'd won the race. Tom grinned at Kai and rolled his eyes, but Kai didn't mind.

"Oh, enough!" grumbled Connor at last. Connor far preferred his own books to Erin's stories, and the two of them often argued.

"Sorry," said Erin. "I thought maybe you

couldn't see the action from so far back!" She laughed loudly, and Connor bristled.

"It's summoning practice tomorrow," he said. "Not that *all* of us need practice. . . ."

Erin scowled. She'd been in the Guild for longer than any of the others, but she couldn't get the hang of summoning Rockhammer. She needed help every time.

"It was a good race," said Kai, stepping in before they started arguing. "Well done, Erin. Rockhammer was amazing."

Erin, still annoyed, made an effort to smile. "Thank you," she said. "Boneshadow did well too." Then she brightened. "Hey, did I ever tell you all how I met Rocky?"

"Only about twenty times," muttered Connor, but Erin ignored him and told her story. Kai listened patiently. Erin liked telling the story, and Kai didn't mind hearing it again.

". . . and then this huge boulder crashed down onto the house!" said Erin.

Sometimes she exaggerated, and sometimes the details changed. Kai wondered if there was another story Erin wasn't telling, but he kept nodding and smiling.

". . . and when I saw who'd rescued us . . . it was Rockhammer!" finished Erin. She grinned around the table. "What about you, Kai? How did you meet Boneshadow?"

Kai smiled. He could feel the dragon's presence in his mind, listening in. Boneshadow liked the story of how they'd met just as much as he did.

"In a book," he said.

"A book?" asked Mira, frowning.

Kai nodded. "My mom looks after animals.

She treats them and studies them. She knows *so much* about them! And she's got all these books on anatomy and bone structure and things like that. She collects books wherever she goes."

Connor looked interested, despite himself.

"Some of the books are ancient," said Kai. "They've got pictures of animals that don't even exist—griffins, basilisks . . . and *dragons*. She showed me the pictures, and there was one dragon looking out of the page, and—I don't know—there was just something about its eyes. . . ."

He shook his head, remembering. "I couldn't sleep that night. It was like the book was calling to me. I got out of bed, crept downstairs. . . . I could see the book on the shelf, and it seemed to be *glowing*."

He remembered the feel of the old paper, crackling as he turned the pages, and there it was: the drawing, in faded old ink, of a strange white creature with a red flare across her chest. Her mouth was open, showing sharp teeth, but her eyes seemed friendly. She was staring at Kai, and somehow, even though it was impossible, Kai had known she could see him. He'd reached out and stroked down the line of her back with a finger, then stared in astonishment as the drawing stretched its neck, as pale as bone, and blew a tiny puff of breath like a shadow across the page.

Hmm, a voice had said—not out loud, but

inside his head, like a dream. *Bone . . . shadow.*
Yesssssss . . .

"I knew right then," said Kai. "I knew she
was my dragon."

And you were my human, said Boneshadow.

Erin sniffed. "That's nice." She sounded
bored. "Mine was more exciting."

"Of course," said Kai, smiling.

It was the boys' turn to clean up after dinner.
Ellis, Tom, Connor, and Kai finished up, then
made their way back to their dorm. Suddenly
they heard a long, clear horn blowing from the
center of the Hall.

"That's the Gathering Call," said Connor, surprised. "What's going on?"

The boys turned back toward the main buildings. Kai reached out in his mind and called Boneshadow, and she appeared beside him. She stretched her neck and sniffed.

"What's happening?" she asked.

"No idea."

The Chancellor of the Dragonseer Guild, Berin, was standing outside her office. Berin was tall and graceful, with dark skin and white hair. She wore a light-blue robe and carried a staff. She smiled as they arrived. Beside her was one of the king's clerks, Malik. He was dressed in black, with curly black hair. Officially, Malik managed the paperwork needed to run the kingdom, but secretly he was a member of the Dragonseer Guild too. He seemed worried.

Kai looked around as they arrived. Everyone else was there—the other children, Creedy and Daisy, Drun and Hilda. The children had all summoned their dragons except for Erin. Connor's dragon, Lightspirit, was a thin, twisting creature, almost like a snake. Ironskin loomed over Tom, while Pathseeker, Ellis's dragon, stood shoulder to shoulder with Ellis. Mira's strange Flameteller, with his bronze coloring and straight features, stood like a mechanical toy. Beside him were Cara and Silverthief, whose shifting colors seemed to blend into the background. They all waited, curious.

"We're sorry to disturb your evening," said Berin, "but a situation has arisen." She nodded to Malik, and he stepped forward.

"Dragonseers," he called. "You have all been summoned to the Royal Palace . . . *by order of the king.*"

3

THE PALACE

Kai and the others stared at Malik, and there was a buzz of worried chatter. Malik held up one hand.

"Let me explain. You may be aware of a trade negotiation taking place in the kingdom?"

"It's with the Southern Cities," Connor said.

Malik nodded. "Exactly. The kingdom of Draconis is negotiating a new treaty with the city-nations of Borolo and Venn. The king's clerks have been working hard: preparing agreements, making copies, revising, and so on. We're almost finished, and the clerks' division went for a celebration dinner. But . . ." He shook his head. "It seems there was a bad batch of mutton served at the meal, and they've become sick with food poisoning. *All* of them, nearly." He looked irritated.

"There's no one to complete the work. Prince Harald has been leading the negotiations, and he suggested . . ." Malik hesitated. "He suggested we should use the apprentice clerks."

It took Kai a few moments to realize what Malik meant, and then he turned to Tom in shock. Tom stared back, amazed.

KAI AND BONESHADOW

Kai and his friends were dragonseers, chosen and brought to the Guild because they had a unique power: to open a path to the world of dragons and invite a dragon into their world. But the rest of Rivven didn't know that. They thought dragons were a myth—tales to frighten small children, of horrible, fierce creatures who hunted humans.

And so, to the outside world, and even to most of the children's parents, there was a different story. Officially, the children were apprentice clerks, learning a trade to help them in their lives.

And now Prince Harald wanted his apprentice clerks to turn up for work.

"But we can't do that," said Erin, looking alarmed. "I mean, we're not *real* clerks!"

"Certainly not you," muttered Connor. "Can you even read?"

"Shut up!" she snapped, but Berin held up a hand.

"Calm yourselves." Her voice was confident and soothing, and Erin fell silent. Berin smiled at them all. "This is an odd situation, but you *have* been learning your clerk skills. You can all read and write well. You can add columns and create contracts. No one expects you to be experts. Prince Harald just needs you to finish copying some documents. Malik will come with you and look after you all. Think of it as a rather unusual adventure.

"You'll set off first thing in the morning, so take this evening to pack what you need. Make sure your clerks' uniforms are clean. Go to sleep early. Tomorrow you will meet the prince."

She nodded to them, and they were dismissed.

"Sounds exciting!" said Boneshadow as they walked back. "I've always wanted to see the palace."

Kai grinned. "Me too! But I don't think you'll be able to appear much. I'm not sure what King Godfic would say if one of his clerks turned out to be a dragon!"

The next day, the children gathered in the center of the Hall. They all wore their official apprentice clerk outfits, dark-gray tunics and capes. They carried packs with everything they would need: clothes, quill pens, inkpots, penknives, slates, and chalk. Malik was waiting for them. As soon as everyone was assembled, they set off from the Guild Hall, through the great doors and along the mysterious Clockwork Corridors, which led outside. Kai felt the corridors move as they walked, twisting and shuffling ahead and behind, creating an impossible maze that hid the Guild from the world.

They exited through a small door in a tiny,

forgotten cottage in a quiet lane. Malik checked each way, then waved the children out. Finally they stepped into the city of Rivven.

Rivven was the largest city in the land of Draconis. It was a sprawling, thriving place, full of merchants and craftspeople, houses

DRAGON STORM

and inns, blacksmiths, tanners, carpenters, artists, and even farmers, for many small farms and chicken coops were squeezed in between buildings. Rivven was dirty, smelly, loud, busy, cramped, and bursting with life. There were tiny passageways, great streets, smoky corners, and open squares—and above them loomed the Royal Palace, sitting atop a huge hill of volcanic rock.

It was a hazy day in late summer. The sky was blue, and the morning chill had already burned off. It would be hot in the city, but Malik led the children up the winding street to the palace, where the air was clear. As they reached the first gates, Kai gazed down over the city.

KAI AND BONESHADOW

Isn't it wonderful? asked Boneshadow's voice in his mind, and Kai smiled.

"Yes," he murmured. Boneshadow might not be next to him, but they could still stay connected and communicate.

The guards waved them through. The

palace grounds were full of gardens, trees, and famous mazes that opened to the public one day every year. Malik led the children to the servants' entrance around the back.

Kai was a little disappointed at first. There were kitchens, storerooms, and servants' quarters that all seemed quite ordinary to him. Everywhere there was wood and plaster, not gold and velvet. But the rooms bustled with people dressed in white outfits or long gray suits, and the kitchens were full of steam, clattering pots, and the smell of wonderful food roasting over the fire. It was like being inside a vast and complex machine.

Malik led the children to a dormitory where they could leave their things. He then brought them upstairs, past the servants and sculleries, to the west wing of the palace. Placing a finger to his lips, he opened a small door and ushered them through.

Beyond the door was a very grand room, with polished wooden floors and a high, vaulted ceiling. A large, round table was placed in the middle, with three important-looking people sitting around it. Behind them were three smaller tables, overflowing with papers and books, wax and sealing stamps, with three clerks writing frantically. The room was full of the sound of quiet talking and the scratch of pens against paper.

As the children entered, the talking stopped and everyone turned. Kai suddenly felt very exposed, as if they'd walked into the wrong room by mistake. A man at the main table stood and strode toward them.

He looked familiar, Kai thought. He was tall, with flowing blond hair, and was well dressed in a blue suit with gold trim, leather boots, and calfskin gloves. Malik bowed as he approached, and the children did the same.

"My lord," Malik murmured.

And suddenly Kai realized who it was.

"Hello," said Prince Harald. "Welcome to the palace."

4
EXPLORING

"Thank you all for coming," said Prince Harald. "Malik tells me you're well trained in your penmanship and clerk duties. Is that correct?"

Among other things! came Boneshadow's voice in Kai's mind. She sounded amused. But Kai and the others were nervous and didn't respond. Prince Harald smiled.

"Anything you can manage will help," he said. "And when our *official* clerks are feeling better, I look forward to telling them that children did their job!" He chuckled, and the children relaxed. Mira was smiling, Kai realized, and Connor was gazing at the prince in admiration.

"Let me introduce you," said Prince Harald. "Here are the delegates: Lord Smale of Borolo and Captain Bright of Venn."

Lord Smale, a tall, thin, gray-robed man, gave them a slight nod before returning to his notes. On the other side of the table, Captain Bright grinned at them. She seemed quite jolly, with rich red clothing adorned with silver lace. She looked a little like a rich pirate.

"We've been working on this treaty for two months now, and everything is nearly complete," said the prince. "You'll be helping to record the details, make copies, and so on."

He smiled again. "You can see how much work there is!" The clerks at each table glanced up briefly at this and then went back to their frantic scribbling.

Malik stepped forward and organized the children. Cara and Connor took their places behind Lord Smale, and Tom and Kai sat at the Venn table, behind Captain Bright. Erin, Mira, and Ellis sat behind Prince Harald.

Kai smiled at the Venn clerk. "Hello," he said.

The clerk looked up for a moment and,

nodding distractedly, took a page of writing from a stack and pushed it toward Kai. "Three more copies," she muttered.

Kai and Tom glanced at each other. Tom shrugged, and Kai took the page. He got out his ink and quill, sharpened the nib with his penknife, and started writing.

The afternoon was quite boring. The two delegates argued, traded, and discussed obscure tax laws. Behind them, the clerks recorded everything they said, in triplicate. Prince Harald was the representative for Draconis and seemed quite comfortable, cheerfully smoothing out arguments between the others.

Kai enjoyed clerk work, and his handwriting was reasonable. Tom, despite his large blacksmith's hands, wrote neatly and quickly, keeping up with the discussions and treaty changes. Kai glanced at the other children. Ellis and Connor were doing fine. So was Mira, although he knew her page would be covered in ink splatters and crossed-out words, because she often daydreamed and tended to draw little designs for machines in the margins.

Cara's handwriting was small and cramped, as if the letters were huddling together to keep safe. Only Erin was struggling. She didn't like clerk work, and her face was red.

At the end of the afternoon, Prince Harald clapped his hands.

"Well, my lord, my lady," he said. "I think that's a good place to pause for the day, don't you?" He smiled. "We have refreshments prepared, and entertainment for this evening."

The diplomats rose, bowed, and left, and Prince Harald followed them. Malik came forward.

"Well done, all," he said. "Let's get you fed, shall we?"

They followed him to a space near the

kitchens, where the servants sat and ate. It was full of cheerful conversation and jokes. When the children appeared, the adults moved over to make room. Kai's hand ached from all the writing, and he was covered in little splotches of ink.

After dinner, Malik returned them to their dorm in the palace and went off to finish his own work. It was still early, and upstairs they could hear music and dancing. Unfortunately, that was only for the diplomats and the other lords and ladies.

"What do we do now?" asked Tom.

Ellis started scribbling in his notebook, mapping out the parts of the palace they'd seen so far.

"Has anyone been inside the palace before?" asked Kai.

"Once," said Cara. She didn't explain.

"I came close," said Tom. "The first time Ironskin and I flew together. We chased another dragon, the one that had started the fire, remember? It came up to the walls and then just disappeared."

"Perhaps it returned to the dragon world?" asked Ellis, but Tom shook his head.

"There was someone on its back. It *must* have landed somewhere."

"Maybe it snuck into the palace somehow," said Erin. "Through a secret entrance. Hey, it could still be here!"

"Maybe," said Connor, stroking his chin.

No one said anything for a few seconds. They looked at each other.

"We should search for it," said Erin.

Tom grinned. "Yeah!"

"Um, are you sure?" asked Mira. "I don't know if we should be out of our rooms."

"Well, everyone thinks we're just kids," said Connor. "We can explore, and if anyone catches us, we can just pretend we were playing."

Ellis looked up from his drawings. "It *would* be good to see the lower levels of the palace," he said thoughtfully.

I'm not sure about this, said Boneshadow's voice

in Kai's head. Kai frowned. He wasn't sure either; it seemed a risky thing to do on their very first night in the palace. But everyone else was enthusiastic, and he didn't like to let them down. "What do you think?" Tom asked him.

"Okay," he said, shrugging. "Sure."

Ellis showed them his notes. "These are the levels of the palace I know about. Tom said the dragon came up to the east side, under the wall, here. So perhaps there's a way in, down these corridors?"

"Well, let's go and see," said Connor.

They crept out of the dorm. Above them, somewhere in the palace, the party was still going on. The corridors were dim and empty. Cara and Ellis led, heading downward. The corridor became darker and felt older, finally ending at what seemed like a solid wall.

There was no one around. Cara closed her eyes, and with a *swish*, her dragon, Silverthief, appeared. Silverthief could spot hidden things. She sniffed around, then padded quietly at one brick.

"There's something strange here," she growled.

Mira came forward and summoned her dragon, Flameteller. Flameteller also had a special ability: he could *sing* to machinery and hear the machinery sing back. He listened and then started to croon in a soft, silken voice. It sounded like smooth wheels turning.

A section of the wall slid open.

DRAGON STORM

The children looked at each other, half nervous, half excited. The space beyond was almost pitch-black. Connor lifted a burning torch from the corridor wall. By its light, they could see steps leading down.

Connor stepped forward into the dark, and the others followed. Kai's heart thumped. They crept down to a wide space made of huge slabs of stone, covered in lichen. Water dripped, and small stalactites hung from the ceiling. A wisp of cool air that smelled like firewood curled past them.

Ellis looked around, making notes in his book. "I had no idea there was anything here," he murmured. "This must be the oldest part of the palace. It might even be what was here *before* the palace."

"There are bars here," said Erin. Her voice sounded loud and echoey.

Kai looked ahead. She was right. He could see old bars, covered in rust but still strong and thick. *It must be a cage of some sort,* he thought. He stepped forward, and his foot scuffed against something. Reaching down, he picked up a leather pouch. It had a strange symbol on the front—a small fish on a triangle, with a crown above it. There was a heavy object inside, like a bottle.

The leather's dry, said Boneshadow.

Kai frowned. He looked around the cavern, at the damp walls and stalactites, and realized what she meant. The pouch should be wet like everything else, but it wasn't. Why not?

It can't have been here very long.

"I think someone's been here recently," Kai whispered to the others, holding up the pouch. "Look!"

But then a noise came from the other side of the bars. There was a snuffling and growling sound, followed by a heavy *thump*. The sound was coming closer.

Kai stared with the others. Should they run? But it was too late—the sounds were almost on them. In the glow of Connor's burning torch, he saw something stomping toward them. . . .

A *dragon*.

5

THE DRAGON

The dragon was twice as tall as Kai and solidly built. It was red, with green ridges along its snout and eyes that gleamed gold. Near the top of its neck were strange flaps of skin, like gills on a fish. They fluttered as it breathed. Its breath was a long rumble, almost like a growl.

For a moment, the children just stared. Then Kai stepped forward.

"Hello," he said, smiling. "I'm Kai."

The dragon peered at him and then at the others. It seemed suspicious.

"It's okay," said Tom, beside Kai. "We're dragonseers. Look, this is my dragon, Ironskin."

He closed his eyes, and the large dark-red shape of Ironskin formed next to him. She bowed.

"Nice to meet you," she said. "I am Ironskin. This is my human, Tomás."

"Wait," muttered Connor. "If the dragon's here, its dragonseer must be around."

The children and their dragons looked around, worried. But then Cara said, "No— look!"

She pointed to a large chain necklace

hanging from the dragon's neck. It held a jewel pendant, glimmering green in the dim light.

"That's an emerald," she said. "Remember when we found the dragon Jadeheart? He had a jewel like that. It has special magic, to keep a dragon in this world even when their dragonseer isn't around."

As Cara spoke, the dragon sniffed at Kai and Tom and Ironskin. Its nostrils flared. Its behavior was strange, Kai thought. He'd met many dragons, and he liked to study them. Most were quite talkative. Closing his eyes for a moment, he concentrated to summon his dragon. Boneshadow appeared. She studied the flaps of skin on the creature's throat.

"Do you think they are for swimming?" she asked. "Like gills, for breathing underwater?"

Kai wasn't sure. They were quivering—in fact, the dragon's whole body was trembling.

Connor turned to Tom. "Is this the dragon you saw?"

Tom nodded. "I think so."

"Hello?" tried Connor. "Do you understand us?"

"Why is it trapped like this?" asked Mira.

Kai had a nagging feeling they were forgetting something. He glanced around the cave, but there was nothing except ancient flagstones, blackened with soot, and plain walls. The dragon was breathing hard now. Its sides were moving, and Kai thought he saw a glint of something yellow and red through the slits in its throat.

"Hey!" yelled Erin. She stepped forward and banged the bars. "Can you hear us, dragon?"

"Stop! You'll scare it!" said Mira. And the creature did step back for a moment. Then it advanced and opened its mouth as if about to speak.

"Fire!" shouted Boneshadow all of a sudden. "Kai, the slits are for making *fire*!"

The flaps of skin opened, and the dragon drew a mighty breath. Kai suddenly realized the red-yellow he could see was a flame, burning inside!

"Down!" he yelled.

"RRRRRROOAAAAAAAARRRRR!"

A blast of fire burst from the dragon's mouth!

"Ahhhhhhhhh!" shouted the children, scrambling back. Ironskin leaped forward and closed her eyes. The air in front of her shimmered, stopping the flames as if they had hit a glass shield. Kai realized she was using

her shielding power—but even so, he felt the heat scorch his face.

The creature stopped and glared at them. It opened its mouth again and shrieked so loud the children had to put their hands over their ears. It was a horrible sound, full of fury but no words.

"Stop!" tried Tom. "We're not here to hurt you!"

"Get away from it!" shouted Connor. "It's dangerous!"

They fled up the steps, with the creature's shriek echoing behind them. Mira's dragon, Flameteller, sang at the secret panel again, slamming it closed. The dragons quickly faded back to their own world. The children raced back through the corridors, but Cara suddenly stopped.

"Wait!" she hissed. "Someone's coming!"

She dragged them into a hidden alcove. Kai was shoved against the wall, and he heard a noise of breaking glass and felt a sharp pain in his hand.

"Ow!"

"Shh!" Cara put a finger to her lips. The children stood in the shadows.

Footsteps echoed down the corridor, and guards ran past. They wore black uniforms with a silver flame embroidered on their sleeves. They carried halberds with razor-sharp tips. Connor frowned. Cara waited a few seconds after they passed, then nodded to the others.

Connor said, "Those weren't the usual King's Guards. Did you see their uniforms?"

"Come on," said Cara. "Before they come back."

The children slipped away, back to their dormitory and safety.

"Phew!" said Erin, grinning. "That was exciting!"

"*Too* exciting," said Connor. "Why did you bang on the bars like that? You scared it!"

Erin snorted. "It wasn't scared. It was out of control! And *you* were still trying to talk to it."

A sharp pain flared in Kai's hand again, and he realized he was still holding the little leather pouch that he'd found in the cavern. A shard of green glass had poked out of it and cut a nasty gash in his palm.

What is that? asked Boneshadow in his mind.

Carefully, Kai opened the pouch. Inside was a smashed bottle with no label. It seemed to have been full of something, but the liquid had soaked into the leather and spread all over his hands. The liquid was deep blue, and it had mixed with the blood on his hand.

You should clean that right away, Boneshadow said, sounding worried. Kai nodded. He went

66

to wash up, but by the time he reached his destination, the strange liquid had almost gone. To his surprise, there was only a thin cut on his palm.

"Are you okay?" asked Mira behind him.

"Yes," he said, peering at the cut, which was barely visible now. "I'm fine."

"So what do we do?" asked Connor.

"We should tell Malik," said Mira. "And Berin."

"We'll get into trouble," said Cara.

"Maybe." Tom shrugged. "But I've never met a dragon like that. Someone here in the palace is looking after and feeding it. And Connor's right—those weren't normal palace guards."

"Maybe we should go back," said Kai. He suddenly felt full of energy. "Take another look, now the guards have gone?"

Everyone looked at him in surprise. "I don't know," said Mira cautiously. "Perhaps we should wait."

The others agreed. Kai shrugged. His

palms were itching slightly, and he scratched at them.

"Well, let's tell Malik tomorrow and see what he says," said Tom. "We should get some sleep tonight." He grinned. "After all, it's back to more exciting clerk work tomorrow!"

Everyone groaned but nodded. Soon they were back in the dormitory and went to bed. It took Kai a while to get to sleep. He stared into the dark for ages, still feeling that strange, wide-awake energy. When he finally drifted off, he was still scratching at his palms.

6

SUSPECTS

The next day, Kai woke up early. He concentrated, feeling the connection open between his world and Boneshadow's.

Good morning, whispered Boneshadow. *How's your hand?*

Kai examined his hands. His palms were still itchy, but otherwise there was no sign of the cut.

"Good," he murmured. He felt wide awake.

He threw off the covers and went to wash up. He whistled loudly as the water splashed. Behind him, the others groaned as they woke up.

"Ugh," muttered Connor. "What time is it?"

"Time you were up, slow-bones!" called Kai.

The others got ready while Kai waited impatiently. He was eager to start the day. He could still feel that rush of energy from last night.

"Remember, we have to tell Malik what we discovered," said Mira at breakfast. But when they found Malik in the debating chamber later that day, Prince Harald was already there.

"Good morning!" said the prince. They bowed, but he just chuckled.

"I don't think we need to bother with that," he said. "Did you have a good evening?"

The children glanced at each other. "Yes, thank you," said Mira politely. "Very quiet."

"Nothing interesting happened at all," added Erin. Malik gave her a surprised look, but the prince didn't seem to notice anything.

"That's good to hear," he replied. "Listen, there's something I need to discuss with you. Something important."

Kai swallowed. What did Prince Harald know? Had someone seen them?

"Thank you for helping with the clerk duties," the prince said. "We appreciate it. His

Majesty recognizes it. The talks are at a . . . tricky stage." He hesitated.

"My father the king is concerned," he continued. "He has heard rumors. The delegates from Borolo and Venn are here on trade talks, but they may be here for something else. The king believes . . . *I* believe . . . they may want to do us harm."

Kai and the others stared at him. He nodded seriously. "You have heard the stories of dragons, right here in Rivven. We believe they may have come from outside Draconis. My father believes that foreign forces want to use dragons against us."

"My lord, are you sure?" asked Malik. He

seemed astonished. Kai almost laughed but then thought about it. Perhaps this new dragon *was* from another country? That would explain the strange uniforms of the guards. But how could the delegates have kept a dragon hidden in the king's own palace?

Prince Harald shrugged. "We are not sure.

But we must keep vigilant. So, clerks: As you work today, stay alert. And if you see anything suspicious, let me know."

There was a sound at the doorway. Two servants opened the doors, and the other delegates entered. Prince Harald smiled.

"Good morning!" he said cheerfully. They bowed and took their places. The second day had begun.

As Kai worked, he wondered about the dragon. Could it really be part of a foreign plot? Kai examined the Borolo diplomat, Lord Smale. His gray outfit already looked wrinkled. His face was long and tired, and his mouth moved constantly, as if he was chewing on a piece of gristle. It was hard to know what was on his mind. It was hard to know what was on *anybody's* mind in the palace, Kai thought.

Kai shook his head and concentrated on his work. It was more copying, but today he found he didn't mind, and he raced through it. His pen slid smoothly over the paper, neat and fast. His writing was even better and quicker than Tom's, and Kai felt a fierce joy at the idea of beating his best friend. Then he grinned. It wasn't a competition, but if it *had* been a competition, he would have been winning. He grinned even wider.

Malik came to their dormitory after lunch to check on them. They could finally speak to him alone! When they told him of their discovery, his face fell.

"You cannot take risks like that!" he said. "What if you'd been caught? Or hurt, even? What if someone had seen your *dragons*? You heard this morning how King Godfic fears them. What do you think he would have done?"

The children ducked their heads. "Sorry," mumbled Connor. "We thought it was important."

"And it was!" snapped Kai impatiently. Malik raised an eyebrow. "I mean, okay, we shouldn't have done it, but we found the *dragon,*

Malik! Someone is keeping a dragon here in the palace!"

Malik nodded. "Yes." He rubbed his chin. "Well. This afternoon's session is the last this week. Then we'll return to Guild Hall. Don't go exploring again, understand?"

He gave Kai a curious look and left.

The afternoon passed like the morning. The delegates made declarations, the head clerks wrote them down, and the young dragonseers copied them out. Again, Kai found the copying quick and easy, and it was Tom who struggled to keep up. As Kai wrote, he watched Captain

Bright, the Venn diplomat. Kai found himself wondering about her as well. Could she be capable of dangerous deeds? he thought. Could the dragon be hers? Could she secretly be a dragonseer?

At the end of the day, Prince Harald stood up and thanked everyone for their hard work.

DRAGON STORM

Malik led the dragonseers back through the streets of Rivven. They walked down the old, forgotten lane to the tiny cottage, then through the hidden entrance and the winding, changing Clockwork Corridors. Finally they arrived at the Dragonseer Guild Hall.

They were home.

7

POWER

It was good to be back inside the Guild Hall, and Kai and the others breathed a sigh of relief. Boneshadow shimmered into view beside Kai, and he rested his head against her neck.

"Hey, Bone."

"Hello, Kai," she said. Her large mouth curled into a smile. "It's good to see you again."

Then she sniffed at him. "Has something changed?"

Kai frowned. "No, why?"

"It's just . . ." Boneshadow tipped her head, confused. "There's something different about you. Are you feeling all right?"

"Yes, of course!" Kai shrugged. "I feel great!"

"How's your hand?" Kai held it out, and the dragon sniffed again.

"That's strange," she said at last. "I was sure the glass had cut into the muscle."

Kai laughed. "Sorry to disappoint you!" Boneshadow was fascinated by human anatomy, just as Kai was interested in dragon anatomy, but today she just seemed to be worrying about nothing. Kai shook his head. "Really, I'm fine. Stop worrying."

The other dragons had appeared too. Kai looked at Silverthief, who was murmuring to Cara. "Silverthief did a good job of finding the hidden passage, didn't she?" he said to Boneshadow.

"Yes," she agreed, still examining Kai's hand.

Kai frowned. "And Flameteller worked the secret mechanism, and Ironskin protected us from the flames." He studied Boneshadow. "You don't really *have* a power, do you?"

Boneshadow blinked in surprise. "Well, we don't know what it'll be yet, do we?" she replied. "Remember what Drun taught us."

She lifted her head and, in a voice surprisingly like Drun's, declared, "No one knows what a dragon's power will be, but it'll be somethin' you need, and it'll happen when you need it."

Kai chuckled. "Yeah. Wish it would hurry up, though." He gazed at Boneshadow and, for the first time, had a rather unusual feeling. Boneshadow was kind, and she was good at caring for people. But she was a bit . . . *boring*. And she was always worrying about things.

The dragon smiled at him, pleased with her impression of Drun, and Kai shook his head. What a strange thought! Boneshadow was his dragon, and he was her human, and that was all that mattered.

"Dragonseers!"

They looked up. Berin was waiting for them. For once, she wasn't smiling.

"Welcome back," she said. "Malik has told me about your adventures in the palace." She looked disappointed. "I'm sure he's already explained what a terrible risk you all took. You must not do that again. Do you understand?"

They nodded. "Hmm," she said. "Well, it is done. And there is a dragon in the palace. We don't know anything about it—how it got here, whose it is, even its name. We know someone is using an emerald charm to hold it in our world. And we know that, for some reason, it is very hostile. It breathes fire. It is incredibly dangerous."

Connor said, "King Godfic thinks another country could be using dragons against us. Maybe someone from Venn or Borolo?"

Berin nodded. "His Majesty has been talking a lot about different countries recently. He seems convinced their leaders are a threat." She pursed her lips. "Perhaps. And yet this must be the dragon Tomás saw months ago. Has it really been here all this time, without anyone knowing?" She sighed. "I'd rather not send you back to the palace, but that would look suspicious. Malik told me you are needed for two more days. So after this weekend you will return to the palace and complete your duties. *Only* your duties. Understood? Let Malik know if you see anything suspicious, but do *not* go exploring again."

She gave them a stern look, but then her expression softened. "Malik says you did your work well and Prince Harald was impressed. So go—enjoy your weekend, relax, and soon we'll be done." She chuckled. "Go! Shoo! Have fun!"

The children laughed and headed away. But as Kai and Boneshadow left, Kai glanced at Berin over his shoulder. She was talking with Malik, and she looked worried.

The next day, the dragonseers relaxed with their dragons. Ellis and Cara went off to explore more of the old ruins at the back of the huge hall. Mira, Connor, and Tom were tinkering with some new invention of Mira's, and Erin had gone to Drun's hut to get help summoning her dragon, Rockhammer.

Kai wandered around with Boneshadow pacing next to him. He wasn't sure what to do. He felt strange, as if he wanted to run and shout, do something energetic, but he couldn't figure out what exactly. Energy coursed through his body. His hands were itching again, wanting to move.

"Whose dragon do you think it is?" he asked. "The one in the cage?"

Boneshadow shook her long head. "I don't know. None of us recognize it. It didn't seem to want to talk. Or maybe it can't?" She blew a breath. "Berin says we should try to forget it for now."

"Hmm." That was probably sensible, Kai thought. But he wasn't feeling very sensible this morning. He nodded to Erin as she came back from Drun's hut with Rockhammer beside her.

"Hey," she said. "You up for another race?"

"A rematch?" asked Kai.

"A chance to catch up," she said. "If you can!"

Kai and Boneshadow exchanged glances, and Kai grinned. "We'll leave you in the dust!"

They headed over to the racetrack, with Kai on Boneshadow and Erin on Rockhammer.

"Ready?" asked Erin excitedly. "Steady . . ." Rockhammer leaped forward. "Go!" shouted Erin over her shoulder.

"Hey!" spluttered Kai. He felt a sudden, unusual surge of anger. *Cheating!* he thought. *Cheating again!* Well, it wouldn't help them— this time he and Boneshadow were going to win, no matter what!

Boneshadow chased after them. Kai held on tight, and the energy roared inside him.

8

WINNING

They raced along the track. Rockhammer's huge legs pulled him and Erin ahead. Kai wasn't worried; the big dragon would get tired later and slow down. He tucked his head down against Boneshadow's warm neck as she powered forward.

They raced around the first bend and into a long straightaway. Rockhammer was still pulling ahead a little, and Kai dug his heels into Boneshadow's sides.

"Ow!" she complained. "What are you doing?"

"Go faster!" he shouted. "They're getting away!"

Boneshadow grumbled but sped up, and at the second bend they were only a few feet behind. Some of the other children had stopped to watch, and behind them stood the gray-robed figure of Vice Chancellor Creedy. Kai ignored them and held on tight.

They hurtled along the next straightaway and the next after that. Rockhammer was tiring now, and Boneshadow started to catch up. As the last turn approached, they were almost level. Rockhammer had the inside line. They could do it!

As they reached the last turn, Erin shouted something to Rockhammer. Kai couldn't make out her words, but suddenly he started drifting outward, into Boneshadow's path! He was trying to force them into a wider turn, Kai realized. What to do? If he moved out, he'd break stride, and Erin would win. But if he kept going, they would crash. . . .

This was what Erin had done before, he thought. In the last race, she'd blocked to make Kai give way. And he had, hadn't he? As the two dragons thundered on, Kai realized that he *always* gave way. He was always the one letting others win, or putting things away for them, or doing what they wanted. Always giving way, always being *nice*. . . .

The energy crackled inside him, and he snarled. He held on tight to Boneshadow and *heaved* her into Rockhammer's path.

Boneshadow yelped. Rockhammer was much larger, but he reared back in shock.

"What are you doing?" gasped Boneshadow. "Let go!"

"I'm *winning*!" shouted Kai. "Now, move!"

They pulled ahead, and behind them Kai heard a *crash*. He ignored it. The air swished past, and he laughed with a reckless joy. Boneshadow raced along the last short straightaway, crossed the finish line, and staggered to a halt.

"YASSSS!" roared Kai, punching the air. "We did it!"

He glanced about, but the other children were looking back down the track. Turning, Kai saw Rockhammer and Erin. The dragon was limping, and Erin had a long scrape up one arm. For a moment, Kai felt a pang of guilt. But then he remembered how they'd tried to beat him, and he grinned.

"Thought you had me at the last turn, didn't you?" he crowed.

"Are you hurt, Erin?" asked Boneshadow. She sounded concerned. "Rockhammer?"

Kai hopped off Boneshadow's back and laughed. "That's what you get for trying to cheat!" he said loudly.

Tom came forward, looking worried.

"Hey, take it easy," he said, giving Kai a strange look. "They had a bad fall back there."

Kai shrugged. Vice Chancellor Creedy approached, and Kai looked up at him. "How was that, *sir*?" he asked, feeling pleased with himself. "Better?"

Creedy studied him. "It was certainly unlike you."

"Maybe I've just decided not to be a push-over anymore," Kai said.

"Indeed." Creedy nodded, but his eyes didn't leave Kai's, and he seemed to be thinking of something else. By now, Erin and Rockhammer had come over to them.

Kai grinned. "That makes us even," he said. "Want a tiebreaker?"

Erin looked down at her injured arm and patted Rockhammer's side. "No," she said in a quiet voice. "Well done, Kai."

She turned and walked away.

"Kai, why are you acting this way?" demanded Boneshadow. "That was really dangerous. Someone could have been badly hurt!"

Kai shrugged. Now that the excitement of the race was over, he felt irritated. He'd beaten Erin at her own game, but no one was celebrating! Even Boneshadow wasn't supporting him!

"Kai," said Tom. "Are you okay?"

"Of course I am!" snapped Kai. "I won, didn't I? But Erin had to make it all about her again. Just because I wouldn't let her have her way!"

Boneshadow said, "I'm really starting to worry about you—"

"Oh, just shut up!" he yelled. Boneshadow stared at him in hurt astonishment. After a second she faded out of sight, back to her world.

Kai stomped back to the dorm, ignoring the others. That was it, he thought. No more being the nice one. No more letting people take advantage of him. He was going to stand up for himself. That's what he'd done in the race.

And that's what he was going to do from now on.

Later that evening, Kai lay in his bunk, staring up at the ceiling.

Dinner had been awkward. The ones who hadn't seen the race had heard about it. Erin's arm was bandaged. Nobody talked much. It was the boys' turn to clean up, but Kai had walked away and left the others to do it. They owed him, he thought. How many times had he been the one left doing the work?

Kai could hear the others snoring, but he was wide awake. At last he crept out of the dorm. He climbed up onto the roof, to a spot where the children often liked to sit, and stared out at the Hall.

It was dark. The magical globes that lit the ceiling of the Dragonseer Guild Hall were dim, like a glimmer of moonlight. Nothing was moving. No one else was awake. Kai leaned against the stonework and scratched his hands.

He didn't summon Boneshadow. He didn't want her nagging him again about the race or worrying about the cut. He hadn't told her the whole truth about that. The cut was gone, but the strange itch was still there, and not just on his hands—the feeling stretched all the way up his arms. Like Boneshadow, Kai knew quite a lot about medicine, and at first he'd been worried it was an infection. But it was on both hands, not just the cut one. Besides, it didn't actually feel *bad*. It was quite exciting— like the tingle of being in a competition, but all the time. He felt great.

And there was something else he hadn't told Boneshadow.

He always knew when Boneshadow was around. He could feel their connection in his head. But now, as he gazed up at the darkness, he felt something else. It was another creature—wilder, fiercer, more powerful. He knew, somehow, that it was the dragon in the palace. He knew it was a he, and that he wanted to get out of his cage. He knew that dragon wanted to breathe fire again. He was dangerous—and exciting! And somehow Kai was now connected to him.

Kai sat on the roof of the dorm, watching the darkness, and smiled.

9

BACK AT
THE PALACE

The next morning, Kai woke up and thought about his strange dream. But . . . had it been a dream? Or had he really sat on the dorm roof in the middle of the night? Had he really felt another dragon out there? The *palace* dragon?

He shook his head and opened the connection to Boneshadow.

"Hey," he murmured. Boneshadow didn't reply. Kai suddenly remembered how he'd behaved the previous day, and he felt embarrassed and shocked. What had got into him?

"Sorry, Bone," he whispered. "I shouldn't have shouted like that. I don't know what happened. I'll say sorry to Erin and Rockhammer too. I promise."

Now he felt that whisper in his mind, and Boneshadow's happy voice.

Thank you. I'm a bit worried about you, Kai.

Kai sighed.

"I'm fine, really." He felt weirdly reluctant to talk about the itching in his arms. He then realized the feeling went all the way up to his shoulders. But he really *did* feel good. He was full of energy, and the world seemed sharper, somehow. There was no reason to worry.

At breakfast he made an effort to smooth things over with the others. Everyone seemed happy to forgive him, even Erin.

"Oh, it's just a scratch," she said, lifting her bandaged arm. "And Rocky's leg is okay too." She grinned. "We'll have that tiebreaker sometime soon, yeah?"

Kai smiled in relief. "Sure."

They had a relaxing day, taking it easy and getting ready for their trip back to the palace. Kai looked up at the cavern roof a few times, trying to recall the sense of the other dragon, but there was nothing.

The following day, as soon as Kai stepped through the servants' entrance and into the palace, he felt the connection again, so strong and clear that he gasped.

Kai, are you all right? asked Boneshadow's

voice. Kai didn't know how to answer. He nodded vaguely, feeling the presence in his mind. It *was* the other dragon! He could feel his strength and rage. And a name. . . .

Firedreamer.

None of the other children seemed to have noticed anything. Kai wondered if he should say something, but a strange instinct told him to keep quiet. He knew something they didn't, he thought. That was a kind of power.

Shaking his head, he followed the others to their dorm.

Firedreamer, he wondered, *what's your story?*

Malik brought them to the debating chamber, and they took their seats. Again Kai found he was racing through the work, better than he'd ever managed before. Even the head clerk seemed impressed. It was easy— he hardly even had to concentrate. He watched the foreign diplomats as they argued over the treaty. Could they be the enemy? Could they be the ones who had brought Firedreamer into the palace?

The day went quickly, and Malik was pleased. The last few details had been sorted. There would be a celebration feast that evening to mark the treaty, then an official signing the next morning, and they would be done.

"I'm afraid lowly clerks are not invited to the feast," Malik said, smiling wryly. "Only the lords and ladies. But I'll make sure the chef sends some food your way." The others cheered, but Kai felt suddenly angry. *Why* weren't they invited? They'd done all the work! Other people were taking advantage of him again! But he didn't say anything. Instead he forced a smile and kept his anger hidden.

"So what shall we do?" asked Erin, once they were back in the dormitory.

"Anyone want to play dice?" asked Connor.

There was a groan from everyone. Connor was excellent at dice and almost always won, although this evening Kai thought he would have a chance. He felt sharp, full of fire, as if his anger was a kind of energy. The itching sensation had spread across his shoulders, now all the way to his chest. He felt as if he wanted to run or shout or fight something. . . .

"We should go back to the dragon," he said.

The others turned in astonishment. "What? No!" said Mira. "Didn't you hear what Berin said?"

"But this is our last chance!" said Kai. "After the signing, we'll be sent home. Don't you want to find out what's going on?"

Tom shook his head. "Kai, we can't."

We can't do that, Kai, said Boneshadow. *Berin said not to.*

Kai shook his head. "I can't believe you all," he said. "We've got a chance to learn something *important,* and you're all huddled here like . . . like cowards!"

Erin bristled. "Hey, I'm not a coward!"

"Kai, what's happening?" asked Tom, looking concerned. "You seem really different. Are you feeling all right?"

Kai stood. "I'm sick of people asking that!" he snapped. "And I'm sick of always doing what I'm told! I'm going, with or without you!"

He stormed out of the room before anyone could react and slipped down the corridor.

Kai, what are you doing?! came Boneshadow's voice. *This is wrong! We have to go back!*

"Oh, stop!" snarled Kai. "You're just like the others, telling me what to do!"

That's not what I mean, started Boneshadow, but Kai shook his head.

"You know what?" he hissed. "I don't think you're even my real dragon. All you do is hold me back. And you can't do *anything*. Firedreamer can breathe flames—did you see that? That's *real* power!"

What? Who's Firedreamer? Kai, listen to me—

"No."

He broke the connection, and Boneshadow's voice disappeared.

Kai grinned. Enough of old Bone! He was going to get a *real* dragon. He moved silently but quickly, scratching at his neck and the itch

that had now reached his head.

10

FIREDREAMER

Kai slipped down the empty hallways, toward the call of Firedreamer.

The dragon's connection was clear in his mind now: a raw, burning power so very different from Boneshadow's. It made Kai want to laugh with delight, but he kept silent, sneaking noiselessly through the corridors.

He stopped at a corner, peered around, and saw a squad of the King's Guard standing at attention. Captain Hork, the head of the King's Guard, was there too, in a shining helmet with a ridiculously tall plume. He was shouting at the others because their breastplates weren't polished enough.

Kai snickered. How different Hork was from the guards they had seen before. How pathetic! He retraced his steps and took a different route. It was easy; he felt as if he had the map of the palace in his mind. Everything was simple now.

He reached the wall with the hidden entrance. Before, they'd needed Silverthief and Flameteller to find and work the mechanism. But within a minute of searching, Kai found the latch that held the entrance closed. The wall slid open, and damp and musty air flowed out. Kai entered. It was still dark, but he could make out the edges of walls and the steps. He could remember the route they'd taken before, down the steps and into the room that was so old it was just like a cave.

The dragon lurked in the darkness, snuffling and growling. Kai stood at the bars of his cage and smiled.

"Come forward," he said. "Come forward, Firedreamer."

Very slowly and cautiously, Firedreamer approached. He stopped at the bars and sniffed the air. He then glared at Kai. His air slits trembled, and he drew in a breath. . . .

"Stop!" commanded Kai. "You won't harm me."

The creature trembled and then blew the breath out again. He bowed his head toward the dragonseer.

Kai grinned. He felt *amazing*. The itch was all through his body now, like bottled lightning, ready to strike. He felt invincible. And Firedreamer was *his* dragon now. Not just a companion, but actually *under his control*. Kai stepped up to the bars. There was a latched bolt, and he undid it.

"Kai!"

Kai turned. Tom was on the steps, holding a burning torch.

"I came to find you," he said. He looked at

the bolt, alarmed. "Kai, what are you doing? Don't let the dragon out!"

Tom rushed down the last steps and faced Kai. A second later, Ironskin appeared. She stood between them and Firedreamer, ready to provide a magic shield.

Kai smiled. "It's okay, Tom. This is my new dragon. His name is Firedreamer."

"Kai, listen to me," said Tom. "It's the liquid—the stuff you got on your hands, remember?"

Kai frowned. "What?"

"That's what Connor thinks," said Tom. "He says it soaked into you. It's affecting you. It's *changing* you. Can't you feel it?"

Kai held his hands up. Nothing was there. Just that strange, powerful itch.

"Something's very wrong, Kai!" said Tom.

Kai stared at Tom and nodded.

"Yes," he said at last. "It's *you*. You're trying to tell me what to do again, just like everyone else—thinking you can order me around. Thinking I'll be *nice*. Well, that's changed."

Kai swung open the cage door.

"No!" shouted Tom.

Firedreamer padded forward, and Ironskin and Tom stepped back. Tom said, "Stay behind Ironskin, Kai!"

Kai laughed. "He's no danger, are you, Firedreamer? Not to *me*, anyway. . . ."

DRAGON STORM

The dragon turned his head toward Tom and then at Ironskin. His nostrils flared as he breathed in.

"Watch out!" shouted Ironskin.

Firedreamer roared! A blast of flame bounced off Ironskin's shield.

"We have to get out of here!" shouted Tom.

Ironskin tried to back up the steps with Tom, but Firedreamer came forward again and blasted another fiery breath. Ironskin was forced to stop and form her shield again. The two dragons squared off against each other, their long necks moving, their teeth bared.

Kai stood to one side, grinning. Firedreamer was so powerful! It was exciting! And yet as he watched, he had a strange feeling. It was

as if it was all happening to someone else. Hearing Firedreamer's roar was wonderful. It was funny seeing Ironskin trying to defend herself! But all the time, he felt as if he could hear someone shouting at him that something was wrong. . . .

Firedreamer leaped forward again, and Ironskin and Tom staggered back.

"This isn't you, Kai!" gasped Tom.

"Maybe it's me now!" shouted Kai. "I'm tired of being nice! I'm tired of you telling me what to do!"

"I'm not!" shouted Tom. "You're my friend, Kai! Please! We're trying to help!"

Kai scowled. No. No, that wasn't right. He was better now. He was more powerful, sharper, and smarter. He didn't need any help! And now he had a powerful dragon, one he could control! But . . . Kai shook his head. The voice was calling to him. He held his hands up again and looked at them. Could there be something wrong? Something inside him, changing him?

Yes! said the voice. *Listen to us, Kai!*

"Boneshadow?" murmured Kai.

Firedreamer shrieked and drove forward. As Ironskin reared to defend herself, Firedreamer swung his huge tail around, smashing into Tom's legs. There was a horrible *crack,* and Tom yelped in pain and collapsed.

"Tomás!" cried Ironskin. Tom had fainted,

and her connection to him was lost. She was slowly fading. "Tomás!"

And then she was gone.

Firedreamer roared in triumph and stomped toward Tom.

Kai frowned. "Tom?" he asked. This was wrong. Something was *wrong*. "Tom?"

He's in danger, Kai!

Firedreamer stood over Tom, snarling, and lifted one huge paw above his head.

"Tom?"

Kai stared at Tom, and just for a moment the strange fog in his mind seemed to part. He suddenly realized what was happening.

"Wait!" he shouted, running forward. "Stop! *Tom!*"

The paw came slamming down.

11
HEALING

"STOP!" shouted Kai, rushing forward. "Move away!"

Firedreamer's paw was inches from Tom's head. He glared at Kai with fierce and wild golden eyes. Beneath him, Tom lay unconscious, with one leg bent at a terrible angle.

"Oh, Tom!" gasped Kai. "What have I done?"

The dragon lifted his paw again.

"NO!" bellowed Kai. He raised a hand. "Stop! I *order* you!"

Kai could still feel the energy coursing through his body. He felt the strange itch in his blood. He could sense Firedreamer and his frustrated fury—and the power Kai had over him. Firedreamer was fighting to break free. The sides of his chest trembled as he breathed. The air slits shivered, and the fire inside his throat flared, ready to roar.

"No!" he demanded again with all his will. "Not my friend!"

Firedreamer hesitated. Then his head dipped, and he stepped away.

"Back!" ordered Kai. "Back in the cage!"

Slowly, fighting every step, the dragon

walked into the cage. Kai slammed the bolt closed with shaking hands and raced back to Tom. What was he going to do? He needed help.

"Bone?" he whispered.

Boneshadow appeared almost immediately. "I'm here, Kai."

Kai felt a wave of relief at seeing her. "Tom needs help!" he said. "He's hurt, Bone, and it's my fault. It's all my fault!"

Boneshadow padded across to Tom and sniffed at his leg. She was bristling, and her shoulders were hunched. Kai suddenly remembered everything he'd said over the last few days. He lifted his hand to his mouth in horror.

"Bone, I'm so sorry! I don't know what's happening!"

Boneshadow turned and scowled at him for a long time. Her face was fierce and grim.

Then, finally, she smiled.

"Kai, you're my human, and I'm your dragon. Whatever's happening, we'll face it together."

Kai let out a shaky breath. "Oh, thank you!" He wrapped his arms around her neck. "I'm sorry!"

"We have to help Tomás," she said. Kai nodded and examined his friend's leg. He knew about dragon anatomy and had to hope humans were similar.

"It's his tibia, I think—his shinbone. It seems

to be shattered." There was a lot of blood. Kai bit his lip. "We could try to carry him, but that could make it worse."

"Kai . . . ," murmured Boneshadow.

Kai closed his eyes. Even now, the power inside him was whispering again, telling him to leave Tom, dismiss Boneshadow, and release Firedreamer. It was a power that wanted to destroy. He pushed it down.

"I'll have to get help," he muttered.

"Kai, wait."

Kai turned. Boneshadow was trembling. She lifted her head. "Kai, I think it's happening. I think this is my power."

"What? Really?"

Boneshadow nodded. Her back arched.

"Keep Tomás steady," she whispered. "Hold his leg."

She peered at the wound. "Yes," she murmured. Softly, she breathed out. . . .

Kai gasped. Beneath his hands, he felt the broken bone in Tom's leg moving! "Are you doing that?" he asked in astonishment.

KAI AND BONESHADOW

Boneshadow breathed again. Now the pieces were reassembling, as if the break was happening in reverse. As Kai stared, the leg straightened and lost its dreadful loose feeling. The skin healed. Soon he could feel the bone, whole again.

"That's really incredible," he murmured. "Boneshadow, you can *heal*!" He remembered complaining about her not having powers, and he felt ashamed. "You have the best power of all."

Boneshadow nodded and looked up at him. "Now you," she said.

Kai blinked. "What?" Then he realized what she meant. The itching was still there.

He was holding it back for now, but it would return—he could feel it. For a moment, he was angry again. He didn't want to lose this power! Boneshadow wanted to take it from him! But he ground his teeth together and stood. This was poison. It wasn't him.

"All right," he whispered.

Boneshadow stood in front of him and breathed her soft breath.

It felt *awful*. As Boneshadow's breath surrounded him, the itch flared up all over his body, so that he wanted to scratch forever. It roared in his head and chest and then his shoulders. Gradually it moved back down to his arms, next to just his hands, and then to the tips of his fingers, like pins and needles.

And then it was gone. Kai let out a loud sob and almost fell over. He felt empty and weak. But slowly his strength came back. And with it, he realized just how wrong the power had felt before. He was himself again, in his own body. It was like coming back home after staying somewhere horrible.

"Thank you," he said.

He reached down and shook Tom's shoulder gently. "Tom?"

Tom muttered something and shivered. Then his eyes opened wide, and he stared at Kai. "The dragon!" he shouted. He looked at Kai in astonishment and then around him and at the cage, barred again. Slowly, his gaze returned to Kai.

"What happened?" he asked. "I thought my leg was hurt."

"Boneshadow healed you," said Kai.

Tom examined Kai. "What about you?" he asked cautiously.

"I'm fine," said Kai. "A bit tired, but back to normal. You saved me." He smiled. "And Boneshadow healed me too." He looked around. Firedreamer was still locked in the cage, growling. But as their eyes met, the dragon seemed to realize that Kai's connection with him was gone. His nostrils flared, and he padded forward again. . . .

"We need to go," said Kai.

Leaning on each other, they staggered up the steps and out of the cave.

12

HEARTBANE

The signing ceremony was very grand. It took place in the Royal Banquet Hall, in front of the king himself. King Godfic gave a short speech, during which he glared at the diplomats from Borolo and Venn as if trying to decide whether to haul them off to the dungeon. Prince Harald spoke next, thanking everyone and wishing them a safe journey home.

DRAGON STORM

The dragonseers watched from a corner of the Hall, where Malik had snuck them in. It was a great honor, but Kai didn't pay much attention. He concentrated on making himself as inconspicuous as possible and didn't look anyone in the face.

He'd told the others the full story. They all said they were happy he was better and were glad no one had been seriously hurt. But they were cautious, and Kai still felt dreadful about what had almost happened and what he'd done.

After the signing, Malik brought them back home. Kai asked to speak to Berin. In her office, he told her what had happened. Berin didn't interrupt or ask any questions. She listened, her face calm, and then asked Kai to wait in the next room.

He waited a long time. Boneshadow kept him company, chatting about the signing ceremony and about how happy she was to be back home. She also talked about her new power and wondered what she and Kai would be doing next. Kai knew she was just making conversation to keep him distracted, but it was nice.

At last Berin asked him to come back to her office. When he entered, Vice Chancellor Creedy and Malik were there too. They looked grim.

"Show me your hands," barked Creedy. Kai blinked and held them out. Creedy brought

out a small blue stone from his robes and
passed it over Kai's fingers, one by one. He
then examined the stone.

"Heartbane," he said at last. "As we
suspected."

Berin sighed. "I wish you had told us, Kai.
We could have helped."

"I didn't really know what was happening," said Kai. "I still don't."

"The vial of liquid you found is called heartbane," said Berin. "A powerful and dangerous potion. It is banned almost everywhere. It makes you stronger, faster, sharper . . . but its power is destructive. It harms your soul."

"When the vial smashed, the potion was absorbed into your skin," said Creedy. "Foolish boy not to tell us. Did you think the way it disappeared was normal?"

Kai shook his head. "I'm sorry," he said. "I know I'll have to leave."

Berin frowned. "Leave?"

"Well, yes," said Kai, surprised. "I mean—

I hurt Erin and Rockhammer. I broke the rules. I almost got Tom killed!"

Berin nodded. "Hmm. Well, I think we can assume you weren't in full control. Mr. Creedy?"

Creedy scowled. "According to the old texts, a dose of heartbane—a *strong*, dangerous dose—is approximately three drops."

"Three drops," said Berin. "That is a dangerous amount, indeed. You had the whole vial. It should have driven you wild. It should have burned you up, turned you into a monster."

"It did," whispered Kai.

"It did *not*," replied Berin firmly. "Something in you fought it all the way. You held it off for days, and even when it finally took you over, you freed yourself from it when Tomás became hurt."

"That was thanks to Boneshadow," said Kai. "She called to me. She was the one who woke me up."

"And how did Boneshadow reach you?" asked Berin. "A dragon cannot make the connection. *You* must have done it without knowing. When things were at their worst, somehow you reached for help. It was the best thing you could possibly do." She smiled. "Kai, you are a good person. The others will forgive you because none of this *was* you. Now, tell me—can you still feel this other dragon, this Firedreamer?"

Kai tried, but he already knew the answer. He'd been trying since last night.

"No."

"Heartbane has another use," said Creedy. "When it is combined with certain magic, the old books say it can give you power to control a dragon."

"Someone at the palace is holding him prisoner," said Berin. "They are using an emerald charm to prevent him from returning to the dragon world, and heartbane to control him."

"It's monstrous," said Malik. He looked furious.

"Indeed," said Berin. "And very dangerous.

Tell me, Kai, is there anything you saw that might help us identify who is doing this?"

Kai thought. "King Godfic thinks it's someone from Venn or Borolo," he said.

Berin pursed her lips. "Perhaps."

"Oh, there was a crest!" said Kai, suddenly remembering. "On the leather pouch. It looked like a fish, I think. Can I have a piece of paper?" Berin passed one across, and Kai drew the shape, as well as he remembered it: a small fish on a triangle, with a crown above it.

"Does that help?"

Berin studied it and glanced at Creedy.

"Yes," she said carefully. "Thank you, Kai. I think we need to consider this." She smiled again. "Well, you may return to the others."

Kai left, and Boneshadow appeared again. She leaned her head against his.

"Poor Firedreamer," said Kai. "I wish I'd taken the emerald pendant off him. Imagine being held like that, not even able to go back to your own world. Do you think that's why he's so wild?"

"It very well could be," replied Boneshadow. "There's something very wrong. The way he is in this world doesn't feel right." She shook her head.

They walked toward the hut where the dragonseers ate. Kai hesitated as they reached the door.

"It's all right, Kai," said Boneshadow. She faded out of sight, but he could still feel their connection. *I'm here with you.*

Kai smiled and nodded, then entered the hut. Everyone was there, chattering, but when Kai came in, they stopped and gazed at him. He blushed.

"Um," he said. "Look, I just . . . I wanted to say I'm sorry—"

"Move over," said Tom.

Kai stopped. "What?"

"Not you, her," said Tom, and poked Erin. "Move over and make a space."

Erin made room for Kai. She grinned at him. "Better be quick. Hilda's made pies, and I've already had three slices." She scooped up another one. "Make that four," she said through a mouthful.

"So . . ." Kai hesitated. "So it's okay?"

"Don't be silly," said Connor. "We figured it out. Something in the potion changed you. Now you're better."

Mira smiled at him. "Everyone knows you're the nicest of all of us," she said. "That's how we knew there was something wrong."

Kai looked at them. "Thank you," he said shyly. "I just—"

"Oh, sit down!" ordered Erin. Kai sat next to her. She thumped him on the back so hard he almost tipped over into a bowl of mashed potatoes. "Eat! Get your strength up. Because tomorrow I'm going to *crush* you in another race."

Kai smiled. "Maybe." He wondered, though. It was great to be back to normal, but perhaps he *had* been a bit of a pushover before? It had

  151

felt good to win! Perhaps next time he'd give Erin a surprise.

"Maybe," he said again. Grinning, he picked up a slice of Hilda's famous pastry pie. "Or maybe not!"

13

EPILOGUE

"Connor," asked Kai after dinner, "have you ever seen this before?"

He drew the shape he'd seen on the leather pouch. Connor peered at it. "Hmm, looks familiar. What's it from?"

"It was on the pouch," said Kai. "Berin thinks whoever owns the pouch is the one holding Firedreamer."

Connor fetched an old book and thumbed

through it. "Here," he said, pleased. "It's something called the Seal of Culon."

He read the article. "It says Culon was the first king of Draconis after the Dragon

Storm. This was his personal seal. It's been passed down to his descendants ever since." He stopped reading. "Wait, this can't be right."

"Descendants?" asked Mira, looking on.

Kai frowned. "But that means . . ."

"That means it was *our king's* pouch," said Cara. "King Godfic's pouch."

"It's the king," said Kai. "It's been the king all along."

"King Godfic is the dragonseer!"

THE DRAGON STORM IS COMING.

Soar into adventure with dragonseer
Erin and her dragon, Rockhammer!

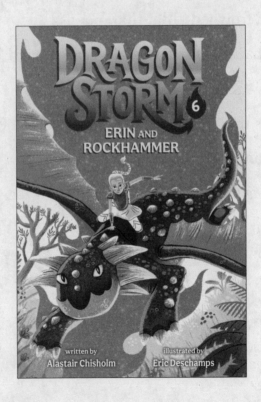